Jenkins Group, Inc.
121 E. Front St., 4th Floor
Traverse City, MI 49684

Special Sales Network
Tel: 616-933-0445
Fax: 616-933-0448
E-mail: rande@northlink.net

Little Lessons f S0-AWM-881

by Mary Kay Shanley

Sta-Kris, Inc.

Marshalltown, Iowa

Printed and bound in the Republic of Korea

Printed by Dong-A Publishing and Printing Co., Ltd.

Published by Sta-Kris, Inc.,
P.O. Box 1131, Marshalltown, Iowa 50158

ISBN 1-882835-31-X

Introduction

I know with certainty that teaching is not an easy task. When I began to work with teachers and did some teaching myself, I realized that "those who teach learn twice" — and we are all better for it! Those who excel as teachers seek new ways to spark the imagination of their students while challenging themselves to improve their skills and enhance their own knowledge.

The greatest gift we can give a child is a
caring teacher. I hope this collection of wisdom,
some simple and some profound, will inspire
you to create those teachable moments wherein
the joy of learning is found.

Other books by Mary Kay Shanley

APPLESEEDS — *Thoughts for Teachers*

SHE TAUGHT ME TO EAT ARTICHOKES
The Discovery of the Heart of Friendship

It's never too late for learning.

1• Yesterday's students learned facts. Today's students learn how to learn. That, obviously, changes the whole notion of how you must teach.

2• Look around. Life-long learners well may be the most interesting people you know.

3• Bulletin boards talk.

4• Along with the "teachable moment" comes the ability to teach it well.

5• Seeing you as a human being may be the most valuable lesson your students learn. Teach them carefully.

6• There's nothing wrong with saying, "No."

7• Never allow your doubt to stand in the way of your success. And never allow your students' doubt to stand in the way of their success.

8•   Make your classroom fair for girls and for boys.

9•   New students are like artichokes. You don't know what's in their hearts until the layers are peeled away.

10•   Set daily, weekly and monthly goals for you and for your students.

11• Children are whole people, just like adults, only they are usually shorter. Remember that.

12• Be as excited about learning as you hope your students are.

13• When a question puts you on the spot, answer it with another question.

14• If you journal every day, soon it will become as routine for you as eating your breakfast.

15• Tell students the only dumb question is the one which isn't asked. Then tell them that again.

16• Never make a threat you don't intend to keep.

17• Subscribe to *Instructor, Good Apple, School Safety* or *American School and College* – or to all of them.

18• It's not that some children don't want to rise to certain expectations. It's that no expectations have been set for them.

19• If you believe students should read, be their best example.

20• Give a youngster who doesn't like to share a copy of *THE GIVING TREE*.

21• A child's first and best teacher should be the parent. Pay special attention to children for whom that's not the case.

22• Don't assume that everybody else is on your wavelength. Outline your position clearly.

23• Be able to give, as well as to receive, constructive criticism—the kind that emerges from respect and concern.

24• Make time for friendship.

25• The best way to teach children to write is by writing yourself. Write in front of them, every single day.

26• Go for a bike ride. (And wear your helmet!)

27• If there's one person in your building who needs TLC, it's the sub!

28• If you strike a bargain with your students, be sure everybody understands the terms of the deal. Then be sure everybody follows through.

29• Mark Twain once said: "The man who does not read good books has no advantage over the man who cannot read them."

30• What if your students found out that even you got excited when the school closed because of bad weather?

31• Encourage parents to see themselves as equal partners with you in the job of educating their child.

32• It's fun to teach those students who want to learn and a challenge to teach those who are indifferent to learning.

33• No matter what size students are, you'll hear them best when you look them right in the eye while they're talking to you.

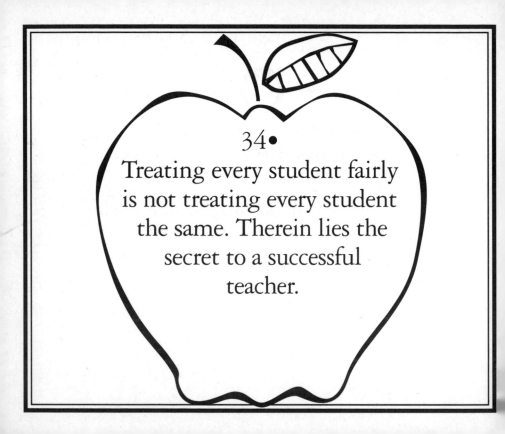

34•
Treating every student fairly
is not treating every student
the same. Therein lies the
secret to a successful
teacher.

35• Hang Christa McAuliffe's picture on your wall. Then put her quote beneath it: "I touch the future. I teach."

36• There's always time for reading aloud. Take 15 minutes to read a biography or three minutes to read a poem.

37• If you get a student who never wonders, charge uphill with the challenge. You've reached a goal when that student finally asks a question.

38• Be on time.

39• Vote in your local Board of Education election.

40• You know that each student in your room is important. But do the students know that about each other? If they do, you'll have a good year together.

41• Celebrate life! Color outside of the lines.

42• Communicate with your peers - openly, honestly and often.

43• Turn off TV for a week. Note how you spend those "extra hours." Then challenge your students to do the same.

44• The United Negro College Fund reminds us that a mind is a terrible thing to waste. However, we shouldn't need reminding.

45• Change the furniture arrangement in your classroom.

46• Reread this quote from Clarence Darrow monthly: "Just think of the tragedy of teaching children not to doubt."

47• Say, "Please" and, "Thank you" a lot!

48•   Heaven: a class discussion where
      everyone shares what they think, and
      where everyone values what their
      classmates shared!

49•   For some students, their only safe haven is
      your classroom. Their only sanity is
      during the school day. Their only warmth
      is your caring.

50• Never underestimate the parent's role in your student's life. No praise is as powerful. No condemnation is as devastating.

51• Never set higher standards for your students than you set for yourself.

52• The lessons students learn today -about successes and failures – will influence them throughout all of their tomorrows.

53• Every time you think you've been stretched as thinly as possible, take inventory. You'll probably find a bit more elastic rather than a tear in the fabric.

54• Don't you think that every month should be Teacher Appreciation Month?

55• If you haven't painted a picture since grade school, paint one now. Who knows what creative juices lurk behind that brush!

56• Ask for help.

57• Greet each parent warmly and sincerely at conference time. Parents may be even more nervous than you.

58• Create a problem with no apparent solution. Then ask students to solve the problem. They'll probably come up with more than one scenario.

59• Never be sarcastic.

60• If you think CD-ROM is a rock group,
you've got a lot of technology left to learn.

61• Jot down the best knock-knock jokes you
hear at Halloween. Then dole them out,
one at a time, to your students.

62• Here's a challenge: Stay one step ahead of your students on the computer.

63• Wouldn't it be sad if you woke up one morning and realized you were done learning?

64• Celebrate life's little successes with your colleagues.

65• Get a good night's sleep, and eat your fruits and vegetables, just like Mom said.

66• Tell students failing is not falling short of a goal. Rather, failing is not trying to reach that goal in the first place.

67• Never feel that you know enough about any subject.

68• Read your memos, journals and newsletters. But most importantly, read a good book for the fun of it.

69• Brainstorm for ideas with colleagues and with students.

70• Memorize this quote from Mark Van Doren: "The art of teaching is the art of assisting discovery."

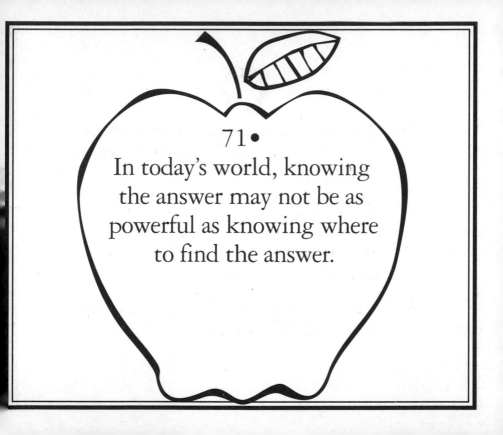

71•

In today's world, knowing
the answer may not be as
powerful as knowing where
to find the answer.

72• Become a student. Sign up for a college course in an area about which you know nothing.

73• There always seems to be a reason why something can't be accomplished. But look around and you also should find a reason why it can be.

74• Teach your students that if they go after excellence, they'll get it.

75• Enjoy your solitude on weekends and get refreshed for the week ahead.

76• Make a note: Do you call on the girls in your class as often as you call on the boys?

77• The best way to teach a child values is to live them.

78• Homework teaches time management.

79• You don't have to like espresso, but you certainly ought to try it.

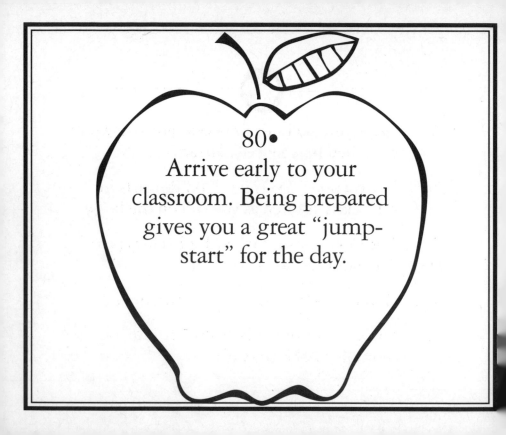

80•
Arrive early to your classroom. Being prepared gives you a great "jump-start" for the day.

81• Questions are our birthright. If we don't know what a child's questions are, at least we know where we must begin.

82• Read to your students, whether they're 6 or 16.

83• Let your students teach.

84• Children live healthier, longer lives if their mothers are literate.

85• The difference between telling students what they think and asking them is that the first method requires them to remember and the second challenges them to think.

86• Remember, students aren't buckets to be filled, but rather they are lamps to be lit.

87• "Read, read, read. Read to discover yourself, not to lose yourself in others' opinions."

Dr. Muhammad Yunus
World Food Prize Laureate

88• If you decide that doing a particular thing in a particular way is unacceptable, don't accept it. Rather, determine first what will make it acceptable.

89• A good walk in the rain can cleanse your soul and your mind, even if you're under a big umbrella.

90• There's a difference between allowing students to look for the easy way and teaching them to look for the challenge. The former may complete a project but the latter turns the world.

91• Learn something new every month. The experience will help you understand your students' frustrations at the beginning of their own new lessons.

92• If you always do something one way, next time do it another.

93• Are you good at teaching? Do you like teaching? Does the world need your teaching? If your answers are yes, yes and yes, you're in the right profession.

94• Allow your students to remind you to be child-like.

95• Occasionally flash one of your knowing smiles. It will either relieve your students or catch them off-guard. Either helps.

96• No student is ever too old for recognition. A simple, "You did very well today," can carry someone into tomorrow.

97• If your definition of failure doesn't imply a second chance, rethink the definition.

98• Students can take in just so much information at one time. Measure carefully the ground you want to cover in each lesson.

99• Plants can transform any classroom into a warm, wonderful place. Start with philodendrons. They're almost impossible to kill, even when you have dozens of garden helpers.

100• If you don't have a team, then you don't have a team. (And that's not good!)

101• People are always more important than things — even people who are doing a very poor job of being students!

102• Think about what you are doing today in the classroom. Will it make a difference for your students in a year? Will it make a difference for them in 20 years?

103• Teachers used to be in the business of serving children. Today, more and more teachers must be in the business of saving children.

104• The best way to teach children to read is by reading yourself, in front of the students, every single day.

105• Monitor progress. Then celebrate success.

106• If you believe that you can make a difference in your students' lives, you're right. If you believe that you can't make a difference in their lives, you're probably still right.

107• Don't stand back and watch your students, dance, sing, laugh and learn. Get out there and dance, sing, laugh and learn with them.

108• Surround yourself with growing things — plants, animals, progress charts.

109• When things aren't going right, remind students of what Thomas Edison said: "I have not failed 10,000 times. I have successfully found 10,000 things that will not work."

110• Take an active role in your building's decision making process.

111• Getting to know someone different from yourself is as good a learning experience as surfing down the information super highway.

112• Every day, every one of us makes a difference. The real power lies in choosing what kind of difference we want to make.

113• Allow your students to make mistakes. Allow yourself to make mistakes. Almost always, breakthroughs will follow.

114• When the class has a roller skating party, be the first one on the rink.

115• Sometimes parents are just like their students. They need encouragement, too!

116• Is there ever a child who cannot learn? Or is it simply that there is a child whom we don't know how to reach and teach?

117• Build a tower of strengths - your students' strengths, your parents' strengths, your colleagues' strengths and your own strengths. You may be surprised at how high that tower will reach.

118• Make mistakes okay.

119•
Make your first
communication with parents
— written or verbal —
positive.

120• When you get up tomorrow morning, the **VERY FIRST THING** you should do is believe in yourself. (Do that even before you brush your teeth!)

121• If you think a pat on the back would make your day go better — and if no one's around to give you that pat — give it to yourself.

122• It takes an entire village to educate the child. And today's villagers are business persons, church and community leaders, parents, senior citizens and neighbors.

123• Look carefully at each of your students today. What will they be 25 years from now?

124• Write a letter to parent volunteers, thanking them for their time and interest in all students.

125• Bake a cake and leave it — with paper plates and napkins — in the faculty lounge.

126• Your work today develops the people power of tomorrow.

127• Make a banner announcing that "Something Good Is Happening In This Room." Then hang that banner across your wall.

128• If you decide each morning to be the best teacher possible that day, you'll probably achieve your goal.

129• Attend the next parent meeting in your school. It sends a strong message that you value their time and effort.

130• Invite grandparents and non-parents to open house. It's one way to involve the whole community in supporting your school.

131• Planting the seed is only the beginning.
Every field must be watered and
cultivated before there's a harvest.

132• Invite parents into your classroom to
teach a mini-lesson.

133• Always have a Plan B.

134• Send a thank you note to every person on your support staff. Include a package of peanuts and say you're just nuts about each one of them.

135• Initiate a swap day where students become the teachers, teachers become the students, and everybody becomes a learner.

136• Share statistics on how well your class is doing collectively by sending a fact sheet home to parents.

137• Put a suggestion box next to your classroom door. Encourage students to jot down ideas to benefit the class. (Tell them "extended vacations" are not a good idea.)

138• Just because certain children are very bright doesn't mean they can —or should — learn by themselves.

139• If you're in a civic organization, tell them that donating books to your school media center would be a marvelous project.

140• Though you may not hear it everyday, so many parents are silently thanking you for a job well done.

141• Can you name any other profession that touches so many people with such long-lasting effects?

142• Learning sometimes can be pretty messy.

143• Ask every teacher in your building to write down his or her four best teaching tips. Put the tips in an envelope and route it among the staff.

144• Give yourself one completely unscheduled day every month.

145•
Don't tolerate insults about
being either a boy or a girl as
"harmless bigotry." Insults
are never harmless.

146• You are an encourager, a planner, a motivator, a counselor, a friend and a helper. (No wonder you're tired at night!)

147• "I've honored myself and the entire family of man by becoming a teacher."

Pat Conroy, Prince of Tides

148• Never, ever tell someone you are "just a teacher."

149• Drop a note to one of your favorite retired teachers, thanking that person for a job well done.

150• Look around your building. Decide who the best teacher is. Then figure out why.

151• Don Shula once said, "Success is never final. Failure is not fatal."

152• Children and their mothers are usually more enjoyable when you don't have them at the same time.

153• Get certified in CPR.

154• You have the power to empower your students. Get them to take risks, build self-esteem and experience achievements.

155• It's far better to develop a reputation as a good teacher based upon what you do rather than upon what you intend to do.

156• Sign up for a class or read a book on how to reduce stress. That's better than fretting.

157• Wouldn't those students be surprised to learn that teachers crave vacation time!

158• You can best teach your students how to care for others by first caring for them.

159• Lucky is the child to whom you give responsibility every day! Lucky, too, is the child whom you recognize for achieving something every day! (Suppose they go hand-in-hand?)

160• Celebrate diversity!

161• Participate in volunteer activities that
   make you feel good about yourself. You
   will get more than you give.

162• Fun is a serious learning opportunity.

163• Sometimes, let your students set the pace
   and provide the direction.

164• "Don't talk to me about potential. Talk to
   me about performance."   Ara Parseghian

165• Teaching is a gift that lasts a lifetime. It grows in value and pays dividends which reach far beyond your classroom.

166• Just as you remember your special teacher, may you be that special teacher whom your students remember.

167• Write down your goals. Seeing them on paper helps make them happen.

168• No subject has to be boring!

169•
Even though you may only
hear from the most vocal,
remember that each student
in your class wants — and
needs — some of your
time.

170• Teaching requires both resiliency and flexibility.

171• Embrace new approaches to teaching. But embrace them thoughtfully.

172• Every morning, get up your spirit as well as your body.

173• A good teacher remembers three important words: Persistence! Persistence! Persistence!

174• If you look into a student's eyes when speaking to him or her, the message you're sending is, "I really care about talking with you."

175• Tell your students too much too quickly and they'll tune you out.

176• Never betray a confidence.

177• Putting things away instead of putting things down will save you hours of searching later on.

178• If you offer students a creative climate, they'll think, work and stretch to be their best. (And so will you.)

179• Seize every opportunity for additional training in your job.

180• Creating plans and following schedules increase effectiveness.

181• Your students are learning just like you do — step by step, a little at a time.

182• By speaking your thoughts out loud, you can teach your students how you think.

183• Help struggling students understand that success is theirs the minute they decide that they want it.

184• Someone always is looking at you as an example of how to act. Don't let that person down.

185• Students aren't the only ones who should learn. Get on a path of continuing study and personal growth.

186• Make it a habit to stretch for a new plateau. (And enjoy that stretching!)

187• If you think MTV is loud, stand in the middle of the cafeteria at lunchtime.

188• Listen with your eyes as well as your ears.

189• For 30 minutes every day, read something just for fun.

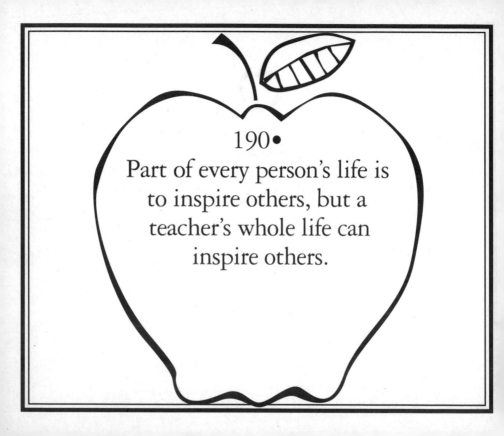

190•
Part of every person's life is
to inspire others, but a
teacher's whole life can
inspire others.

191• If one approach to a lesson doesn't work, head in another direction.

192• Make it a habit to be creative.

193• School was not a good experience for some parents. So just like their child, they could benefit from a little hand-holding.

194• Nobody knows better than you that the problems education faces today are different from the problems education faced yesterday or probably will face tomorrow.

195• Listen to books on tape on the way home from work.

196• Don't issue idle threats to students who need disciplining.

197• Think about today before you go to sleep tonight. Then decide how you can make tomorrow better.

198• A student who is afraid to fail will have little chance of succeeding.

199• Curl up on the davenport tonight and listen to classical music.

200• Make your daily schedule realistic.

201• Ask your students to jot down notes on a big THANK YOU! poster. Then give it to the custodian.

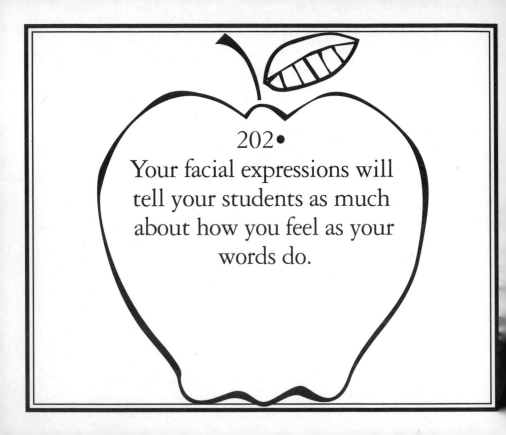

202•
Your facial expressions will tell your students as much about how you feel as your words do.

203• When your students are doing well, share in their exuberance.

204• After your class completes a tough project, get everybody to join in a round of applause.

205• At the beginning of each school year, give parents a tip sheet so they can help their children be better students.

206• The one thing most everyone wants to hear on the first and last day of school is the closing bell.

207• Each student has something to teach you. Listen and learn from everyone in your class.

208• Since you spend 40 percent of your time listening, make sure you listen well.

209• Attend your students' activities —
basketball, orchestra, the play. That sends
a message that you care 24 hours a day.

210• Set your watch five minutes ahead so
you're never late for an appointment.

211• Learning sometimes can be pretty noisy.

212• Tonight, sit back, relax and give your
mind a chance to probe.

213• As much as possible, delegate classroom responsibilities to your students.

214• Think of yourself first as a learner. Then you will become a better teacher.

215• Call parents more often about the good things their child does than about the bad things.

216• Thinking and speaking aren't necessarily simultaneous exercises.

217• Know the difference between nagging and nudging.

218• Always expect the unexpected.

219• The same thing happens to the best laid plans of mice and men as it does to those of teachers.

220• Share good ideas with your colleagues.

221• New teachers should spend as much time as possible observing in other classrooms.

222• Ever worry that when the end of the day comes, you won't recognize it?

223• Like it or not, you're a role model.

224• Don't make your gifted students into teacher assistants. They need to learn new material, too.

225• Look for the individual within each of your students.

226• Call every student by his or her name, every day.

227• Enroll in a course on origami.

228• Encourage students to follow their passions.

229• Find out each student's strengths. Then find out if that student is aware of those strengths.

230• Students know the important stuff — like which teachers really care.

231• Never, ever let an opportunity slip past you.

232• Your students will relate to your enthusiasm before they'll relate to you.

233• Always consider the effect of your actions on the student's self-esteem.

234• Laugh with — never at — your students at least once a day.

235• "All you should ask of anyone — that they attempt to contribute." Rod Steiger

236• When you draw up your "Things To Do" list, stay realistic. (There are still only 24 hours in a day!)

237• Your favorite question of students should be, "Why?"

238• Some people quit work at 5 o'clock and don't work again until the next morning. Imagine that!

239• Lecture less. Discuss more. Question often.

240• A good teacher loves to teach others to love learning.

241• All teaching requires is wisdom, prudence, broad shoulders, perseverance, caring, a love of laughter . . .

242• A truly special teacher sees tomorrow in every student's eyes.

243• A school is a Kid Zone: Enter with care and patience.

244• Maybe the reason some students don't rise
to the challenge is because they've never
been expected to.

245• To teach is to touch a life for the rest of
that life.

246• Your best memories as a teacher will
never be erased.

247• Hugs are healthy.

248• If you do something pretty effectively, think about how you could do it very effectively.

249• Some days, teaching is like being in a blender with no off-button.

250• Take the time to reflect and teach your students to do the same.

251• When is recess?

252• Has anyone seen my desk?

253• No child wants to be a "bad" student.

254• Give your students the freedom to explore.

255• Technology cannot accomplish more than you program it to accomplish.

256• In the best lessons, the teacher always learns more than the students.

257• There's no such thing as a substitute for a good teacher.

258• You learn from the past, share the present and teach for the future.

259• You don't always need to be everyone's best friend, but you always need to be friendly.

260• Set deadlines.

261• It seems like vacation should be here pretty soon!

262• Invite your students into your world. Tell them about you!

263• Smiles are contagious.

264• Since we teach listening skills to our students, can we teach listening skills to ourselves?

265• Go to the Friday night ball game and sit where the students can see you.

266• Grade papers promptly.

267• Never return a students writing project without telling the student what was done right and what could have been done better.

268• The hardest thing to find in the teacher's supply cabinet is time.

269• Ahh — yet another fund-raising chili supper!

270• Once a month, invite a community resident who has expertise in an unusual area to talk with your students.

271• Sometimes, a troubled student's silence says more than that student's words ever could express.

272• "I hear and I forget. I see and I remember. I do and I understand."   Chinese Proverb

273• Studying a foreign language teaches students not only new words but also new worlds.

274• Students will do what you genuinely expect them to do.

275• Be "other" centered and your students will be, too.

276• If you're enthusiastic about what you're teaching, your students will be enthusiastic about what they're learning.

277• Wouldn't your students be surprised —
on that opening day of school — to learn
that you're as nervous as they are!

278• That student in your room who is the
most difficult may also be the one who
needs you most.

279• Students learn from what you do, not
from what you say.

280• Always greet your students with a smile!

281• Give your students confidence to be competent.

282• Grade yourself.

283• Be daring. Ask your students how they think you're doing as a teacher!

284• Do your best. It counts!

285• Make education a part of your dreams.

286• Be a life-long learner yourself.

287• Respect within the teacher-student relationship is a two-way street.

288• Walk your talk.

289• Every student should produce published work every year.

290• Variety is the spice of life — and nothing is more full of life than a classroom.

291• There never should be a question about who is in charge in the classroom.

292• A parent-student-teacher conference involves the whole team.

293• A suggestion to Mom or Dad: Refrigerators actually were invented to display your student's work.

294• Meeting often with peers encourages consistency among teachers.

295• Parenting and teaching go hand in hand. (Or at least, they should go hand in hand.)

296• Make technology in the classroom your slave.

297• Make communicating with parents part of your routine.

298• If your student's family doesn't have a phone, send letters to the parents frequently.

299• A room rich in print encourages learning.

300• Cherish consistency. Follow through with rules, enforcement and consequences.

301• Keep a journal of your thoughts, ideas, fears and joys.

302• If life is amazing (and it is) and if you're a teacher (and you are), then be ready to serve as a conduit to that amazement.

303• Mediocrity should be neither a standard nor a goal.

304• If you spot a pedestal today, climb up on it.

305• You are a professional.

306• The brilliant teacher may be appreciated, but the one who touches our human side is loved.

307•
" Spoon feeding, in the long
run, teaches us nothing but
the shape of the spoon."
E.M. Forster

308• Every student has the right to learn something new every day.

309• Your reputation as a teacher says a lot about who you are as a person.

310• Some people think teachers have a life outside of the classroom. (Where did they get that idea?)

311• Some people think you're done working by mid-afternoon!

312• Some people think elementary teachers are actually comfortable in those little chairs.

313• You can never learn anything while you're talking.

314• Expect respect from your students, and settle for nothing less.

315• "Learn not to sweat the small stuff."

Kenneth Greenspan

316• "Good teachers know when to let us go.
And this is almost always before we feel
ready to be on our own."   Christopher Clark

317• Tell students that school is like a game,
with rules to be followed.

318• In the classroom, one size does not fit all.

319• Being flexible may be more important than being organized, especially when letting go of plans takes you in a new, exciting direction.

320• Accept students as they are, not as you wish them to be.

321• Lucky are the students whose principal wants to know what the teachers think.

322• A teacher ignites the flame of learning. A student keeps the flame burning.

323• Where does the wind shift more than in the fields of education?

324• Establish a means of communicating with parents — through newsletters, parent-teacher journals, phone calls or Friday folders.

325• Every student in your room believes that he or she is the most important student in that room. Good for all of them!

326• The students who are your biggest problems are the ones who need you the most.

327• Remember the people from your past whom you treasure most. What they were has made you what you are.

328• Remember blackboards?

329• Learn from and with the students.

330• Talk with, not at, the students.

331• Be courageous. Show your imperfections.

332• Sitting for long periods of time can cause
Buttock Fatigue.

333• Organization is an art form. Some achieve masterpieces while others are still finger painting.

334• A bad day is when merely going around in circles sounds productive.

335• The odds of making a positive difference are in your favor.

336• A teacher who gives freely of himself or herself is a teacher who is totally committed to the endeavor of teaching.

337• Being prepared for the expected is your job. Being prepared for the unexpected - that teachable moment - is your challenge.

338• For some students, the easiest thing to wear is guilt.

339• Speak softly but carry a big bottle of aspirin.

340• "Over the long run, superior performance depends on superior learning."   Peter Senge

341• Think today.

342• Model friendship for your students.

343• Tell students not only when you've learned something new, but how you learned it.

344• What if the first thing you felt each morning when you woke up was an excitement about the day ahead?

345• "Education shouldn't compete with
national defense, the trade deficit, drugs
or AIDS. Instead, think of it as a solution
to those problems."   David Kerns

346• If you play chess, form a student chess
club.

347• Ask your students to evaluate their own
work.

348• When the school closes because of bad
weather: sleep in; read a book; clean out
your storeroom. (Scratch that last idea!)

349• Learning is like a pair of shoes: everybody
needs them, but the size, comfort and fit
vary from one person to another.

350• Set a clear policy on homework — why
it's expected; how much time it will take;
how parents can help.

351• Ever wonder why they call it "hot" lunch?

352• Education is not an expense. It is an investment.

353• Encourage creative thinking by expecting your students to be problem solvers.

354• No two students are alike, so what is the point of comparing them?

355• Good teaching is really the art of suggesting.

356•
It's important to know your stuff. But it's even more important to know whom you are stuffing.

357• Read students' favorite books over and over. It's like visiting an old friend.

358• If you allow it, the students will become the best judges of their own work.

359• Rewriting is as much a part of the writing process as writing.

360• If you and your students want to have some control of the future, plan for it.

361• What if, as a teacher, you actually had time!

362• Don't measure your students by how often they fail but by how often they succeed.

363• Ever notice that the most successful students in school often have the most involved parents.

364• You should be afraid of what you don't know. But you never need be afraid of what you do know.

365• Try to look upon life's little trials as little.

366• Who was your favorite teacher when you were growing up? And why?

367• Remember when you thought teaching would be fun because teachers knew everything?!

368• A student whose bad habits are pointed out consistently will continue to work on perfecting them.

369• All children can learn, but each child has his or her own learning style.

370• It's hard to look beyond the student who demands attention toward the student who doesn't. It's also necessary.

371• Most teachers have two offices. One is their classroom. The other is their dining room.

372• Every time you begin a sentence with, "They say that . . . ," stop and ask yourself who "they" are anyway.

373• See beauty in your students.

374• The best way for a student to get out of difficulty is to go through it.

375• Students aren't the only ones who should take a time-out just to play.

376• Teachers are trimtabs, those small devices on rudders that allow huge ocean vessels to change directions.

377• Invite senior citizens in to share what life in your community was like when they were children.

378• If you don't know anything about ballet, go to a performance. Then at least you'll know whether you like what you saw.

379• Respect your students. They should settle for nothing less.

380• Even if you could teach responsibility, loyalty and caring from a textbook, modeling those attributes yields a far stronger lesson.

381• Decide who's the best teacher you know. Then trade that person a free meal for an evening of their wit, wisdom and philosophy.

382• What if, at the end of each day, your students could do something they couldn't do that morning?

383• Never tell the new teacher on staff everything you know about the job.

384• Success is when you're able to raise both the floor and the ceiling.

385• Tell students it's easier to do something right than to do something over.

386• A little pat on the back never hurt anyone — not even a teacher.

387• It's easier to nourish healthy grass than to go around digging out the weeds.

388• Remember when you thought teaching
would be fun because you would have
summers off?

389• Did you know that, all too often, gifted
students become drop-outs?

390• What if every graduate knew how to
change a car tire!

391• Never take yourself on a guilt trip. The
scenery is depressing, and when you're
through, you still haven't been anywhere.

392• Imagine if a student told you that he or she wanted to become a teacher because of you.

393• Experiencing that unexpected, teachable moment is your joy.

394• If you want to test the waters, remember to keep one foot on the shore.

395• Bring a plate full of hors d'oeuvres to the faculty lounge. Who cares if it's a weekday morning!

396• Check out some "how-to" videos at your library and become your own handyperson.

397• It's easy to focus on yourself. It's better to focus on others.

398• If a student doesn't rise to the challenge, perhaps the work is too easy rather than too hard.

399• For some students, the easiest thing to place is blame.

400• Know the difference between a pat on the back and a pat on the head.

401• "The only things worth knowing are things that allow you to know something else; they are generative."   Ted Sizer

402• Put each student's name on two index cards; shuffle the cards; call on a student only as his or her name comes up.

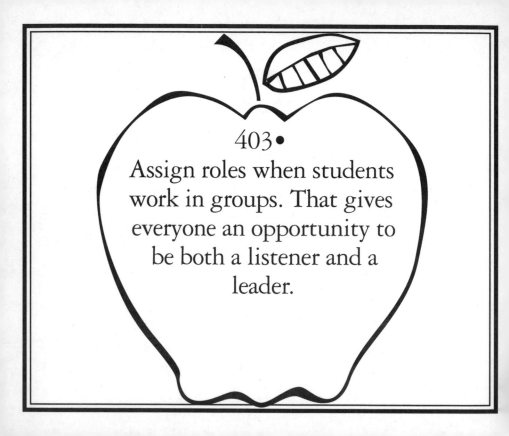

403•
Assign roles when students work in groups. That gives everyone an opportunity to be both a listener and a leader.

404• In the morning, call on students who volunteer the answers. In the afternoon, choose students who don't raise their hands.

405• Homeless students aren't as concerned with progress reports as they are with a place to sleep at night.

406• The more your community understands what you're trying to accomplish, the more community support you'll have.

407• Ask if some of your students can present one of their projects to the Board of Education at their next meeting.

408• Take the whole class outside today.

409• "Thinking is the hardest work there is, which is probably why so few people engage in it."   Henry Ford

410• Students who don't know they can't will attempt the impossible. (And maybe they'll achieve it.)

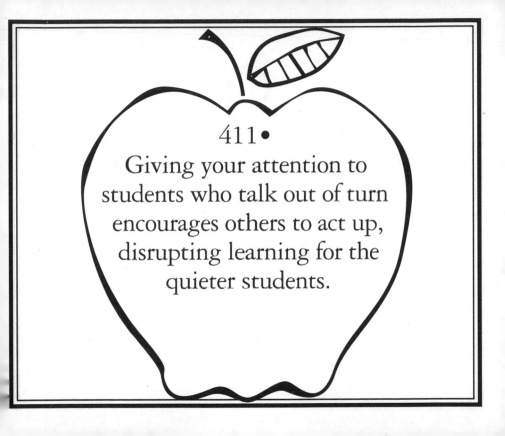

411•
Giving your attention to students who talk out of turn encourages others to act up, disrupting learning for the quieter students.

412• No lesson in any subject has to be dull.

413• Discuss with students, but don't decide for students.

414• You may have computers, a television, fiber optics and interactive video in your classroom, but you are still the teacher.

415• You may be a good teacher, but even YOU can't teach a student who is hungry.

416• What if everyone in the school's parking lot actually parked within the lines?!

417• Ask yourself why it is that boys almost always do better than girls in math and science.

418•
Remember when you thought teaching would be fun because then you'd get to go into the faculty lounge?

419• Mentor a new teacher. (Remember how you felt?)

420• Develop your own methods for handling frustration. Then practice them!

421• If somebody invents little control knobs that we can put on our tempers, they'll need to come in children AND adult sizes.

422• Being indifferent is a curse.

423• Resilient people — those who succeed
     despite adverse circumstances — almost
     always have someone who believes in
     them. Be that one person.

424• Teachers are those persons who develop
     overwhelming urges to stand up in the
     movie theater and demand that everyone
     be quiet!

425• When a student gets discouraged, say,
     "You will learn this." That student needs
     to know you believe in him or her.

426• Students don't learn something by listening to you talk about it. They learn by saying it themselves and applying it to their world.

427• Nobody is born fearing mathematics.

428• Do tomorrow's lesson plans today.

429• Read UP THE DOWN STAIRCASE. Then decide whether anything has changed since that book was written.

430• Civilizations are remembered by their wars and their fine arts. We have a choice. If we choose the former, we destroy. If we choose the latter, we create.

431• Remember when you had to clean the erasers instead of clearing the computer screens?

432• The more methods you use to assess a student's performance, the more you understand that student's abilities and knowledge.

433•

Our schools are our future.
How well you and your
students do today will
determine how well all of
us do tomorrow.

Dear Teacher,

If all of us work together to make a difference for students, that difference will happen. One way to move in that direction is by sharing our tips, wisdom and advice with one another. I welcome your thoughts about what it takes to be a good teacher. Please write to me:

Mary Kay Shanley

P.O. Box 1131

Marshalltown, IA 50158